Every new generation of children is enthralled by the famous stories in our Well Loved Tales series. Younger ones love to have the story read to them. Older children will enjoy the exciting stories in an easy-to-read text.

British Library Cataloguing in Publication Data

Ainsworth, Alison
   The emperor and the nightingale.—(Well Loved Tales).
   I. Title   II. Russell, Chris   III. Andersen, H. C. Nattergalen
   IV. Series
   823′.914[J]   PZ8
   ISBN 0-7214-1054-5

First edition

Published by Ladybird Books Ltd Loughborough Leicestershire UK
Ladybird Books Inc Lewiston Maine 04240 USA

© LADYBIRD BOOKS LTD MCMLXXXVII
All rights reserved. No part of this publication may be reproduced, stored in a retrieval system, or transmitted in any form or by any means, electronic, mechanical, photo-copying, recording or otherwise, without the prior consent of the copyright owner.

WELL LOVED TALES

The Emperor and the Nightingale

retold for easy reading
by ALISON AINSWORTH

illustrated by CHRIS RUSSELL

Ladybird Books

Once upon a time, in the far away country of China, there lived a powerful Emperor.

The Emperor had a magnificent palace. It was built of the most delicate porcelain, and filled with marvellous treasures.

The palace was surrounded by beautiful gardens. The splendid flowers that grew there had tiny silver bells, that tinkled as you walked past.

Beyond the gardens lay a wood, and beyond the wood was the sea.

In a tree that grew close to the water's edge, there lived a nightingale. How sweetly that nightingale could sing! Even the poor fisherman who cast his nets under the branches of her tree, stood still to listen to her song.

Travellers came from all corners of the earth to visit the Emperor's palace. They admired his fine treasures, they marvelled at the splendid flowers in his beautiful gardens. But if they were lucky enough to hear the nightingale sing, they all agreed, "This is the best of all."

Many books were written about the Emperor's palace and its treasures. And it was always the nightingale that was praised above all else.

These books were sent all over the world. One of them reached the Emperor.

The Emperor was pleased as he read the fine descriptions of his palace and gardens.

Then he read something which surprised him very much. The words "But the nightingale is the best of all" were written in the book.

"What in the world is this?" he cried. "Can there be such a bird in my very own garden, and I have never even heard of it?"

He called his Prime Minister.

"There is said to be a most remarkable

bird here, called the nightingale," said the Emperor. "They say her song is worth more than all my treasures. Why has no one told me about her?"

"I have never heard of her," replied the Prime Minister, "but I will go and look for her."

So the Prime Minister searched the palace. He ran upstairs, downstairs, along corridors, through many halls and countless rooms.

He asked everyone he met about the nightingale. But nobody had heard of her.

The Prime Minister returned to the Emperor, and said, "Your Imperial Majesty should not believe everything that is written in books. The person who wrote about the nightingale must have made it up."

The Emperor replied, "But the book was sent to me by the High and Mighty Emperor of Japan, so it must be true. If I don't hear the nightingale singing *this evening*, the whole court shall be punished."

In great alarm, the Prime Minister searched the palace once more. Most of the court searched too. Nobody wanted to be punished.

At last they met a little kitchen maid.
She said, "Every evening I take food to
my mother, who lives by the sea. On the
way, I often hear the nightingale singing.
It is so beautiful, it makes me cry!"

The Prime Minister ordered the little kitchen maid to lead him to the nightingale. Most of the court went too. They were all curious to see this marvellous bird.

On the way to the sea shore, they heard
a cow mooing.

"Listen," said a page boy. "It's the
nightingale! What a deep voice she has!"

"No," said the little kitchen maid.
"That is a cow. We must go a little
further."

They passed by a small pond, where a frog was croaking.

"I can hear her now!" cried a courtier. "Her voice sounds just like church bells."

"No," replied the little kitchen maid. "That is a frog croaking. But we shall soon hear the nightingale herself."

At last they came to a tree close to the water's edge. The little kitchen maid pointed to a small bird sitting on a branch.

"There she is," she whispered. "The nightingale."

"Could it be possible," asked the Prime Minister, "that such a plain creature could sing so beautifully?"

"You shall hear for yourself," replied the kitchen maid. "Dear nightingale!" she called in a soft voice. "Please sing for us."

And the nightingale sang so sweetly that everyone was enchanted.

"It sounds like glass bells," sighed the Prime Minister. "How strange that we have never seen or heard her before."

Then he said, "Most excellent nightingale! I have the honour to invite you to sing before his Imperial Majesty,

the Emperor, this evening."

"My song sounds far better among green trees," replied the nightingale. But she wanted to please the Emperor, so she agreed to go to the palace.

A golden perch was placed in the middle of the grandest hall in the palace. The whole court had gathered there. Even the little kitchen maid was allowed to stand by the door.

All eyes were on the small bird as she settled on the golden perch.

The Emperor nodded his head as a signal for her to begin.

25

The nightingale sang so sweetly that tears of happiness filled the Emperor's eyes and rolled down his cheeks.

He said, "The nightingale shall have my golden slippers, and wear them round her neck."

But the nightingale replied that she had seen tears in the Emperor's eyes. That was the greatest reward she could have.

Then she sang again in her sweet, lovely voice.

From that day, the nightingale lived in a golden cage in the palace. She could fly out twice during the day and once each night.

Twelve servants held a strong silken rope fastened to her leg.

There was not a man, woman or child throughout the Empire who did not talk about the wonderful nightingale.

One day a clockmaker brought a present
for the Emperor. It was an artificial
nightingale, made of silver and covered in
diamonds and other precious stones.

When the bird was wound up with a tiny silver key, it sang one of the real nightingale's tunes. As it sang, its tail, all glittering with gold and silver, moved up and down.

The Emperor was delighted with his new nightingale. He put it next to the real bird, so that the two could sing together. But, while the artificial nightingale always sang the same song, the real one sang different notes each time.

The clockmaker told everybody that his

nightingale was even better than the real one.

"With the real nightingale you never know which song she will sing next," he explained. "*My* nightingale always sings the same song and you know it will always be perfect."

So the artificial bird sang on his own. His voice was as beautiful as the real nightingale's, and he was much prettier to look at.

He could sing his song thirty times over and never be tired. The whole court listened and watched with delight.

Then the Emperor declared that he
wished to hear the *real* nightingale sing
once more. But where was she? Nobody
had noticed her fly out of the window,
back to her green woods. They had been
too busy admiring the artificial bird.

"Well, what an ungrateful nightingale!" cried the Prime Minister.

"She shall be banished from the Empire," ordered the Emperor. Then he carried on admiring the artificial nightingale, and soon forgot about the real one.

The artificial bird had his own silken cushion close to the Emperor's bed. All the presents he had received, gold and silver, lay around him.

A year passed. The Emperor, the court and all the people of China knew every note of the artificial nightingale's song. They all loved to sing along with the bird.

One evening, the Emperor was lying in bed as usual, listening to his nightingale. Suddenly there came a loud "bang" from inside the bird, followed by a strange whirring sound. Then the music stopped.

The Emperor jumped out of bed. He summoned the clockmaker, who took the bird to pieces and mended it as best he could. But the tiny wheels which made the notes were wearing out. From that day on, it was not safe for the bird to sing more than once a year.

Five long years passed. Then the Emperor fell ill. He lay, cold and pale, in his great bed. Thinking that he was already dead, his courtiers hurried away to greet the new Emperor who was waiting to take his place.

But the Emperor was not yet dead. He could feel a heavy weight on his chest. Opening his eyes, he saw Death sitting on his heart. He had the Emperor's crown on his head, and the Emperor's golden sword in one hand. In the other hand he held the imperial banner.

Strange faces peeped out from behind
the banner. Some were very ugly. Some
were kind and gentle. They whispered
about the good and bad deeds the
Emperor had done during his life.

The Emperor was terrified. He called to his courtiers to beat the royal drum so that he couldn't hear the fearful whispers. But his courtiers were not there.

He commanded his artificial nightingale to sing, but the bird remained silent. How could he sing with nobody there to wind him up?

So the Emperor had to listen to the terrible voices, going on and on.

All at once the sweetest sound was heard from outside the window. It was the real nightingale! She had heard that the Emperor was dying, and had come to pay her respects.

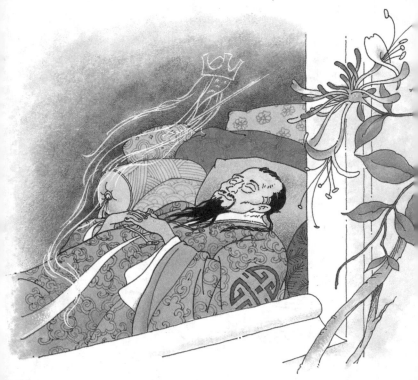

As she sang, the awful faces vanished behind the banner. Then the nightingale sang of the quiet churchyard where Death had his home. Like a cold white shadow, Death flew out of the window and returned to his churchyard.

The Emperor felt much better. He sat up. Tears of happiness shone in his eyes.

"Thank you, dear nightingale," he cried. "I banished you from my Empire, yet you returned to save me from Death. How can I reward you?"

"You have already rewarded me," replied the nightingale. "I have seen tears in your eyes, as when I sang to you the first time. Now sleep, and I shall sing to you again."

So the Emperor slept peacefully. When he woke the next morning, the nightingale was still singing at his window.

"You shall stay here for ever," said the Emperor. "And I shall break the artificial bird into a thousand pieces."

But the nightingale begged the Emperor not to harm the artificial bird. Then she said, "I cannot live in the palace, but I shall come to your window and sing every evening. I can bring news of all that happens in your Empire. But you must promise to tell no one that I sing to you, and all will be well."

The Emperor promised, and the nightingale flew off into the wood.

Soon the courtiers came in to look at their dead Emperor – and he sat up and said, "Good morning!"